Mom cleaned out the refrigerator. She put an orange peel in the garbage can.

She put a large leaf
of cabbage in the
garbage can.

She cleaned off the
counter and put
toast crusts in the
garbage can.

"Paige, will you help me take the garbage can out to the street?" asked Mom.

"I will in a second,
Mom," said Paige.
"I want to dance in
the grass."

"Paige," called Mom again. "Are you ready to help me?"

"I'll be right there,"
said Paige. "I am just
at the end of my
magic show."

Paige ran back into
the kitchen. "Paige,
are you all set to help
me now?" asked Mom.

Paige ran up the stairs
to her bedroom. "In
two seconds, Mom,"
she called out.

"Ready, now?" Mom
called from the bottom
of the stairs.

10

"I just have to find my gyroscope," Paige said. "It is for my magic show. Will you help me look?"

"I will help you," said
Mom, "but you need
to help me after that."
"Yes, I will," said Paige.

Mom helped Paige
look for her gyroscope.
Paige looked on the
rug. Mom lifted up
scraps of paper on
the desk.

"Paige, here it is!"
said Mom.
"Thanks, Mom,"
said Paige.

"After I help you take
out the garbage," Paige
said, "can I do my
magic show for you?"

"I would like that,"
said Mom. "Let's take
the garbage can to
the street. Then we
will have lemonade
and magic."

16